Lily's Garden of India

Text © 2003 ticktock Entertainment Ltd
Illustrations © 2003 ticktock Entertainment Ltd
Cover Illustrations © 2003 ticktock Entertainment Ltd

First published in Great Britain in 2003 by ticktock Media Ltd, Unit 2, Orchard Business Centre,
North Farm Road, Tunbridge Wells, Kent TN2 3XF

 **Children's Publishing**

This edition published in the United States of America in 2003 by
Gingham Dog Press
an imprint of McGraw-Hill Children's Publishing,
a Division of The McGraw-Hill Companies
8787 Orion Place
Columbus, Ohio 43240-4027

www.MHkids.com

Library of Congress Cataloging-in-Publication Data is on file with the publisher.

Printed in China.

1-57768-491-5

1 2 3 4 5 6 7 8 9 10 TTM 09 08 07 06 05 04 03

The *McGraw·Hill* Companies

Lily's Garden of India

By Jeremy Smith

Illustrated by Rob Hefferan

GINGHAM DOG
P R E S S

Columbus, Ohio

Lily thought her mother was the best mother in the whole world. This was because her mother made everything an adventure, especially the garden in their backyard. It was filled with flowers from all over the world. And each section of the garden featured plants from a different country.

There were flowers from the mountains of India, plants from the lakes of France, and fantastic trees from the rain forests of Africa.

One day Lily found a path she had never taken before, where strange plants shot like fireworks out of the ground.

"Lily! Lily!" a little voice said. "Welcome to the Garden of India.
I am the jasmine plant, and I have a story to tell you."

Lily sank into the soft grass and listened to the little jasmine plant speak.

"We are treasured by the people of India who use us in many of their festivals. Our white and pink flowers decorate the hair of young girls during celebrations and are used to make colorful necklaces."

As the jasmine finished her story, and before Lily had a chance to catch her breath, she heard someone else calling her name.

"Lily! Lily!" a huge voice boomed.
"I am the banyan tree, and I too
have a story to share with you."

Towering above her, the enormous
tree began its tale. "My branches
send great shoots to the ground
that take root and grow,
providing shelter
for passersby."

"I am known as the tree of life. People come to me to meet, think, and make their wishes. Sometimes they even build shrines beneath my roots, where candles stay lit day and night."

As the banyan tree finished his tale, Lily found herself caught up in a whirl of brilliant colors.

"Lily! Lily!"

Lily turned around to hear a group of plants giggling behind her. "We are the marigolds. Listen to our story."

"Our fiery flowers are so beautiful they are given every day as gifts to the Hindu gods in Indian temples. We are also used to mark a Hindu festival called *Diwali*. Every year at this special time, people flock to the holy Ganges River and send our petals spinning out onto the water to give thanks to their gods."

Lily stepped into a waiting boat and floated down the river, surrounded by marigold petals and candlelight.

Soon she found herself in a different part of the Indian garden.

"Lily, Lily!" a wise old voice croaked. "Come and listen to my story. I am the coconut tree, and I have lived in India for over a thousand years. People love to eat my delicious fruit and drink my milk. My leaves are also used to thatch roofs or they are made into thread to help stitch fishermen's boats together."

Lily split open the coconut shell, drank its cool milk, and ate the delicious flesh.

As the sun began to fade, Lily heard another gentle voice calling her. "I am the Neem Tree. Come over here and hear my story. I know you are tired, child, but please come."

Lily made her way over to the friendly tree.
The tree lifted her high into its branches.

"Neem trees are simple trees found throughout India. When the New Year arrives, people celebrate by eating our berries with a delicious treat called jaggery sugar. They do this to welcome all things bitter and sweet for the year ahead."

Lily popped a berry into her mouth and made a face! It tasted so sour!

The neem tree laughed out loud. "Go and drink from the stream, child, to forget the taste!"

As Lily drank, she noticed a crowd
of people gathered around a colorful
tree in the distance.

"Lily! Lily!" a proud voice called.
"I am the mango tree, and my fruit
tastes so good that I am known as the
king of fruit. Why don't you try one and
see what you think?"

Lily took a bite. The mango was delicious, sweet, and juicy! As Lily finished eating, another lovely scent floated across to her on the early evening air.

"Hello Lily," said a little tea plant. "Or as we say in India, *namaste*, which means "hello" and "goodbye." Do you recognize me? I originally came from China, but now I am one of India's most famous symbols."

"Here, I am called *chai*. When you visit the northern highlands, you will be offered a cup as a welcoming gift. It is polite to accept."

Lily was very sleepy and ready to go home, but there was one more plant calling to her.

"Lily! Lily!" called a sweet-smelling flower. "I am the lotus. Close your eyes and listen to my story. I am dedicated to the sun, because I open my flowers at sunrise and close them at sunset. I appear in many beautiful colors, and I am sacred in India. I am also a symbol of purity because, although I grow in the muddiest of rivers, my petals always remain spotless."

Lily breathed in the scent
of the lotus flower and breathed out her tiredness.

As the sun slipped away, Lily noticed
that all the plants were now silent
and at rest.

She ran home along the winding, twisting path. As she ran, she heard another,
more familiar voice calling her name. "Lily! Lily!"

Lily ran into her mother's arms.

"Lily, I have been worried about you. Where have you been?"

"I've been across the world to India, where I have sailed on the Ganges River, walked across tea fields, and stood under a vast tree the size of many houses."

A smile spread across her mother's face, and they both went indoors, thinking of India.

Glossary

Jasmine

This fast-growing shrub or vine has deep green leaves and clusters of fragrant pink, yellow, or white flowers. The flowers last just one day before withering and dying. Jasmine flowers are used in many festivals and celebrations. Valued for its beautiful fragrance, the jasmine's deep red oil is used in many perfumes.

Marigold

Found in Europe, Western Asia, and the United States, this plant is known for its blazing orange flowers. Oil from its petals has been used to treat skin complaints for centuries. The marigold is known in India as a herb of the sun because of its golden color. Hindus use marigold petals for religious purposes, throwing them into the Ganges River during their festival of Diwali. Marigolds can grow to a height of up to 24 inches.

Banyan Tree

The banyan tree is a huge species of fig, with scarlet fruit the size of cherries. Birds pick up the seeds and drop them on the tops of palm trees. The seeds send down shoots that embrace and eventually kill the palms. The shoots then take root, growing up to 3,000 trunks. One banyan tree can create a forest spanning several acres. The banyan's main trunk is more than 40 feet around, but it splits into several trunks as it ages.

Coconut

The coconut tree is native to Southeast Asia and grows along the seashore. Part of the palm family, it has a thin trunk that can stretch up to 100 feet tall. Living in tropical places where the weather is often stormy, the coconut tree grows at an angle that helps it survive strong winds. Its many tiny flowers are a symbol of fertility and prosperity because they signal the coming of many fruits. The flowers eventually turn into the fruit known as a coconut. Inside the hard husks of the coconut are delicious flesh and milk.

Neem Tree

A broad, strong, tropical species, the neem tree can live for over two centuries. It can reach heights of up to 50 feet and survive extreme heat and drought. In the summer, small white flowers bloom that have a jasmine-like scent. The flowers become an edible fruit. In India, people often call the neem the "village pharmacy" because the neem provides so many different cures. Villagers drink the neem tea as a tonic and use the twigs as toothpaste, while local doctors use the juice to treat skin disorders.

Tea Plant

Originally from China, the tea plant is a tough, evergreen bush that can grow up to 6 feet high and wide. Fragrant white flowers bloom in the fall, and shiny fruit grows in the summer. The tea plant, also known as chai, is best known for its leaves. They are harvested and dried to make the famous drink that is enjoyed all over the world. There are more than 3,000 different varieties of tea.

Mango

Reaching heights of up to 130 feet, this beautiful evergreen plant provides valuable shade during the hot tropical summers. As its shiny leaves grow, they change color from red to green. In the summer, the mango grows delicious golden fruits. During the Diwali festival, the blossoms are placed in front of shrines. They are also hung outside homes to bring good luck and to celebrate the coming of spring.

Lotus Flower

The lotus flower is a water lily that covers rivers across India. The exquisite white, yellow, or pink lotus flowers rise above the water and sit on beautiful flat leaves. In the Hindu religion, the lotus represents long life, health, honor, and purity because of its ability to remain spotless and unspoiled in the muddiest of marshes. It is also seen as a living miracle because the seeds of the Indian lotus can germinate 200 years after they are shed. The leaves are edible and can be used as a painkiller.

Indian Festivals

Diwali—Festival of Lights

Diwali falls on the night of the new moon in the Hindu month of Kartik (October/November). The festival marks the victory of light over darkness and good over evil. Presents are given, lamps burn, and fireworks are lit.

Holi—Festival of Colors

Holi is a Hindu festival celebrated on the full moon of the month of Phalgun (February). The meaning of Holi today is to strengthen your faith in God and make yourself a better person. People pray to Krishna—the supreme Hindu god—and sing, dance, and paint each other's faces.

Baisakhi—Harvest Festival

The festival of Baisakhi is celebrated by Buddhists and Sikhs. It falls on April 13th and, in Northern India, marks the New Year. People bathe in holy rivers to cleanse themselves.

Raksha Bandhan—Festival of Brothers and Sisters

This Hindu festival is celebrated on the day of the full moon in the month of Shravan (August). On the day of Raksha Bandhan, sisters tie a decorated thread, called a rakhi, around the wrist of their brothers. This thread symbolizes protection and commits brothers to look after their sisters.

Navratri—Festival of Nine Days

The Hindu festival Navratri leads up to Diwali. Three goddesses are worshipped: Durga (left), the goddess of strength; Lakshmi, the goddess of wealth; and Saraswati, the goddess of knowledge and learning.

Krishna Janmashtami—The Birth Of Krishna

This Hindu festival celebrates the birth of Lord Krishna and falls in August. Krishna was born at midnight, so people pray in temples until the day ends.

Eid-ul-Fitr—End of Ramadan

This Islamic festival is celebrated by the Muslims of India. It marks the end of the month of Ramadan, during which Muslims fast from sunrise to sunset. By forgetting about their appetites, Muslims concentrate on spiritual matters and become closer to God. People wear new clothes, and children receive gifts and money.

Growing Your Own Marigold

Lily is entranced by the blazing gold colors of the Indian marigold. These beautiful flowers can be grown almost anywhere in the world. You can even grow one at home. Just follow these simple steps.

1. Buy a pack of marigold seeds from a gardening store.

2. Fill a pot to the top with gardening soil or a good potting soil. Ask someone at a garden center to help you choose the right type of soil.

3. Open your pack of marigold seeds, and plant three or four seeds about 1½ inches below the surface. Place them 4–6 inches apart from each other.

4. Marigold seeds need the warmth of the sun, so place your pot in a spot where it will get lots of indirect sunlight—for example, on a windowsill or a table in a sunny room.

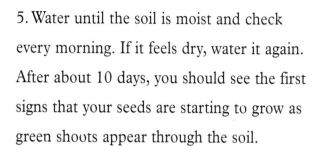

5. Water until the soil is moist and check every morning. If it feels dry, water it again. After about 10 days, you should see the first signs that your seeds are starting to grow as green shoots appear through the soil.

6. After 6–8 weeks, your plants should be 6–8 inches tall. In the spring, you can plant them outside in a flower bed or garden where they will grow even bigger. Choose a position where the marigolds will get lots of indirect sunlight.

7. In the summer, your marigolds will grow into golden flowers.

8. In the fall, the flowers will die. Crack them open to find seeds inside. You can plant these again next spring and enjoy a fresh crop of marigolds!

Namaste
"Goodbye"